For sweet dreams . . .

Copyright © 2003 by Kim Lewis Ltd.

First U.S. edition 2004

Library of Congress Cataloging-in-Publication Data

Lewis, Kim, date.
Good night, Harry / Kim Lewis. —1st U.S. ed.
p. cm.
Summary: When Harry, a toy elephant, has trouble sleeping, his friends help him.
ISBN 0-7636-2206-0
[1. Bedtime—Fiction. 2. Sleep—Fiction. 3. Friendship—Fiction. 4. Toys—Fiction.
5. Elephants—Fiction.] I. Title.
PZ7.L58723 Go 2004
[E]—dc21   2002041468

2 4 6 8 10 9 7 5 3

Printed in China

This book was typeset in Berling.
The illustrations were done in colored pencil and pastel.

Candlewick Press
2067 Massachusetts Avenue
Cambridge, Massachusetts 02140

visit us at www.candlewick.com

Good Night, Harry

Kim Lewis

CANDLEWICK PRESS
CAMBRIDGE, MASSACHUSETTS

Harry the elephant
was getting ready for bed
with his friends
Lulu and Ted.

"Good night, everyone," said Harry.

"Zzz," went Lulu.

"Snore," went Ted.

Harry lay waiting.

But sleep didn't come.

"I forgot my bedtime story,"

thought Harry.

He opened his books.
He looked at the pictures.

He looked at the words.
His eyes grew heavy.

He snuggled down again.
"I'm waiting," he said.
But sleep didn't
come to Harry.

"Maybe I'm not really tired,"
thought Harry.

He hung up his clothes.   He cleaned up his room.

He ran in place.

He touched his toes.

He hopped on one foot.

He jumped up and down.

Then Harry got back into bed.

"Zzz," went Lulu.

"Snore," went Ted.

"I'm waiting," said Harry.

But nothing happened.

"Maybe I'm not really comfy," thought Harry.

He stretched out
one way.

He stretched out
another way.

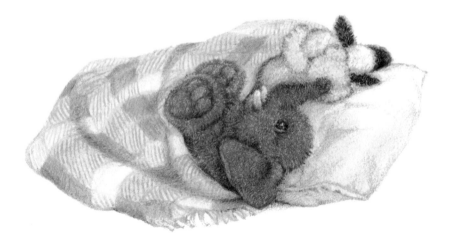

He lay on his tummy.

He lay on his back.

He closed his eyes tight.

"Zzz," went Lulu.

"Snore," went Ted.

"I'm still awake," sighed Harry.

Then Harry began to worry.

He worried and worried.

He just couldn't stop.

He thought of tomorrow.

He thought of today.

He thought about nothing.

He thought about lots.

He wriggled and squiggled.

He rolled in a ball . . .

and he took all the blankets.

"Hey!" said Lulu,
waking up with a start.

"Harry, what are you doing?" asked Ted.

"I can't get to sleep,"
said Harry sadly.

Harry looked out the window.

He rubbed his tired eyes.

"What if sleep never ever
comes at all?" he said.

"Don't worry, Harry," said Lulu.
"We're here, Harry," said Ted.

The three little friends sat close together.

They looked at the world outside.

Lulu sang a song to the moon.

Ted counted the bright evening stars.

They heard an owl hoot.

Petals fell in the breeze.

They felt the dew of the night.

Harry snuggled up
with Lulu and Ted.

His eyes felt heavy.

He gave a big yawn.

"Good night, Harry," said Lulu.

"Sweet dreams, Harry," said Ted.

But Harry was fast asleep,
and "Snuffle" was all he said.